The Berenstain Bears
Lose A Friend

It's sad to lose a friend.
It makes us wonder *why*...
But a family's love and care
can help us say goodbye.

The Berenstain Bears
Lose A Friend

Stan and Jan Berenstain
with Mike Berenstain

HarperFestival®
A Division of HarperCollins*Publishers*

The Berenstain Bears Lose a Friend
Copyright © 2007 by Berenstain Bears, Inc.

HarperCollins®, ♣®, and HarperFestival® are trademarks of
HarperCollins Publishers. Printed in the U.S.A. All rights reserved.
No part of this book may be used or reproduced in any manner
whatsoever without written permission except in the case of brief quotations
embodied in critical articles and reviews. For information address
HarperCollins Children's Books, a division of HarperCollins Publishers,
1350 Avenue of the Americas, New York, NY 10019.
Library of Congress catalog card number: 2007924690
ISBN 978-0-06-057405-5 (trade bdg.) — ISBN 978-0-06-057389-8 (pbk.)
www.harpercollinschildrens.com
❖
First Edition

There are pets and there are pets.
There are dogs and cats that
you can play with and pet.

You can train a parakeet
to sit on your finger.

There are bunnies
that you can cuddle.

There are adorable little chicks that grow up into big ferocious, strutting roosters.

Then there are goldfish—quiet, shy goldfish. You can't play with them, of course. All you can do with goldfish is watch them swim, admire how beautiful and graceful they are, and feed them.

That was fine with Sister Bear. She was very fond of Goldie, her goldfish.

Goldie wasn't necessarily supposed to be just Sister's pet. But that's how it worked out. The other members of the family were on friendly terms with Goldie, but it was Sister who took care of the little goldfish. Not that Goldie needed all that much care. Sister would feed Goldie twice a day, once in the morning and once in the evening.

Sister didn't really expect Goldie to do much except look beautiful and swim gracefully, gently swishing her tail this way and that. So Sister was a little surprised when Goldie came over and sort of said hello when Sister came to feed her. Well, she didn't *exactly* say hello, but she did bump her nose against the fishbowl when she saw Sister with the fish-food shaker.

When the food landed on the surface of the water Goldie would do a little underwater dance, nipping up at the floating fish food.

Every morning Sister would say, "Good morning, Goldie!" and shake the fish food on the water. Then Goldie would bump up against the bowl and do her underwater dance nipping at the food. They did the same thing every evening.

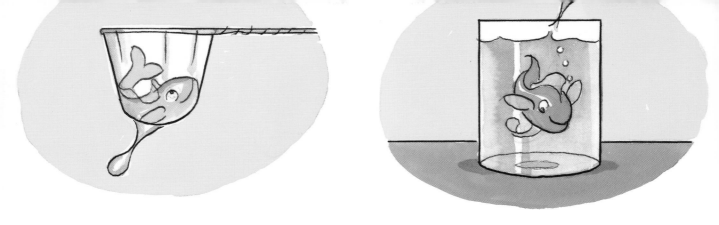

Sister made sure to change Goldie's water and clean her bowl every third day. Sister would carefully scoop Goldie out of her bowl with a little cloth scoop and put her in a glass of clean water. Then she would sponge out the bowl, fill it with clean water, and put Goldie back in her bowl. But Goldie looked so lonely, all by herself in her bowl.

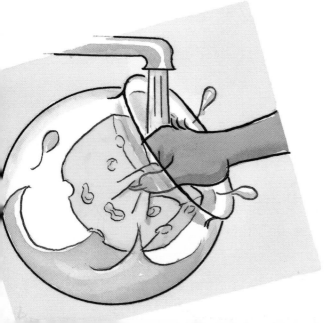

So Sister went outside and got some colored pebbles from the backyard brook.

She brought them into the house, washed them off, and
then carefully dropped them into Goldie's bowl.
They looked very nice as they settled at the bottom.
Goldie seemed to like them. She swam around
exploring them with her nose. The pebbles were
white, pink, gray, and lavender. They set off
Goldie's orange-gold color beautifully.

One day when Mama and Sister stopped off at the pet store for fish food, Sister saw a beautiful fishbowl castle.

"That castle would be just right for Goldie," said Sister. Mama agreed.

Goldie seemed very much at home in her pebble-lined bowl and her beautiful new castle. And every morning Sister would say, "Good morning, Goldie," and Goldie would answer by coming out of her castle and bumping her nose against the bowl. Sister would sprinkle the fish food onto the surface of the water and Goldie would do her underwater dance and nip at the fish food.

Then one day when Sister and Brother
were at school, all that changed.
Mama was straightening the room
when she saw it. "Oh, dear!" she said.
"Oh, dear! Oh, dear!"

There was Goldie floating belly-up in her bowl. "Papa!
Would you please come here a minute!"
cried Mama, sounding upset.
    Papa saw the problem right away.
    "What do you think?"
asked Mama.

"What do I think?" said Papa. "I think Goldie has passed on to the big underwater castle in the sky."

"Oh, my! Oh, my!" said Mama. "Sister will be heartbroken."

"Yes," said Papa. "Sister's mighty fond of that little fish."

"What should we do?" asked Mama. They both thought it over.

"Hmm," said Papa, "I think I have an idea. Why don't I rush over to the pet store and get another goldfish— one that looks exactly like Goldie? It shouldn't be too hard. They all look pretty much alike. That way nobody will be the wiser, and poor Sister won't be crying her eyes out."

"You know, dear," said Mama. "I'm not sure that's such a good idea. For one thing . . . "
But Papa was gone.

There were lots of goldfish in the big tank at the pet store, and they all looked pretty much alike.

"That one," said Papa. "No, not that one. The one next to it." It took a while, but the pet store clerk finally netted a fish that looked for all the world like Goldie.

By the time Sister got home from school, the new goldfish looked very much at home exploring the castle in the pebble-bottomed fishbowl.

But that evening when Sister said, "Good night, Goldie" and began to sprinkle fish food onto the water, the fish didn't bump its nose against the bowl. It stayed hidden in the shelter of the castle. Sister didn't think much of it at the time.

But when the same thing happened the next morning, Sister began to wonder. She became suspicious. She coaxed the new fish out of the castle and looked at it very closely.

Papa and Mama began to get a little nervous.

Then suddenly Sister cried, "THAT'S NOT GOLDIE! THAT IS A DIFFERENT FISH! I CAN TELL BECAUSE GOLDIE HAD A TINY PINK SPOT UNDER HER CHIN AND A TINY BLUE SPOT UNDER HER TAIL AND THIS FISH DOESN'T! WHERE'S MY GOLDIE? WHERE IS SHE?"

"Now, dear, I hate having to tell you this," said Mama. "But while you were at school yesterday, poor Goldie died and . . . "

Sister began to cry. "Where is she?"

"She's in a safe place, sweetie," said Mama.

"And who's this fish?" said Sister.

"Well, your father knew how upset you'd be about Goldie, so he thought it might be a good idea if he went to the pet store and got another fish, one that looked like Goldie and, well, you know . . . "

"Yes, I know," said Sister. "Papa tried to fool me, and it's not right to try to fool someone about a thing like this."

"Gee, don't be too hard on Papa, Sis," said Brother.
"He was just thinking of you."

"I know," she said.

"Here she is," said Mama handing Sister poor Goldie wrapped in a hanky. "You know, dear," she added kneeling down and giving Sister a hug, "Goldie lived a happy life. Goldfish aren't meant to live very long. You took good care of her and she was a good fish."

"I know," said Sister, wiping her eye. "Can I keep the hanky?"

"Yes," said Mama.

"You know those boxes that the kitchen matches come in?" asked Sister. "Could you put the matches in something else and let me have the box?"

Mama put the matches in something else and gave Sister the box. Sister slipped Goldie into the box and closed it. Then she headed for the back door.

GOLDIE

"Er, can I come along, Sis?" asked Brother.
"Sure," said Sister. "And bring a little shovel
and one of those waterproof markers."
"We'll *all* come, okay?" said Papa.
Sister nodded.

So, Sister, Brother, Mama, Papa, and Honey Bear all climbed a small hill behind the tree house. They found a medium-sized rock. Sister wrote something on the rock. They dug a hole, put the box in the hole, and covered it with dirt. Sister put the rock on the little mound of dirt. They stood on the hill for a little while, then headed back to the house.

Sister got to be good friends with Goldie Two,
but she never forgot Goldie.